Gabby's Fair

Written by Robin Klein
Illustrated by Michael Johnson

An easy-to-read SOLO
for beginning readers

SOLOS

Southwood Books Limited
4 Southwood Lawn Road
London N6 5SF

First published in Australia by Omnibus Books 1998

This edition published in the UK under licence from
Omnibus Books by
Southwood Books Limited, 2001

Text copyright © Haytul Pty Ltd 1998
Illustrations copyright © Michael Johnson 1998

Cover design by Lyn Mitchell

ISBN 1 903207 21 5

Printed in Hong Kong

A CIP catalogue record for this book is available
from the British Library

For Brittany – R.K.

For Lorna – M.J.

Chapter 1

Mum was too busy running the plant stall to look at anything else. She just gave Matt and Gabby some money for the fair, putting Matt in charge of it.

"Meet me back here at five," she said. "Make sure you stay together, and have fun."

Being in charge of the money made Matt very bossy.

"First we'll go on the climbing wall," he told Gabby.

Gabby looked scared. "I'll *hate* it."

"Don't be such a wimp. I'll go first, and all you have to do is follow."

"I'd rather have a pony ride …"
Gabby said.

But Matt was already joining the line at the climbing wall.

Chapter 2

Matt wasn't scared. He raced up the wall like a lizard, then sailed down the other side on the rope. But Gabby shut her eyes tightly when her turn came.

"You need them open," said the woman in charge. "So you can see where to put your feet."

Gabby couldn't explain to the woman that her feet felt like two melted icy-poles. They just wouldn't move, and she was holding everyone else up.

Matt had to come and take her out of the line.

"Fancy being scared of a wall!" he said.

Chapter 3

"Can we have a pony ride now?"
Gabby asked in a small voice.

"Not yet. Maybe after we go on
the ferris wheel."

The ferris wheel played nasty tricks, like stopping when they were

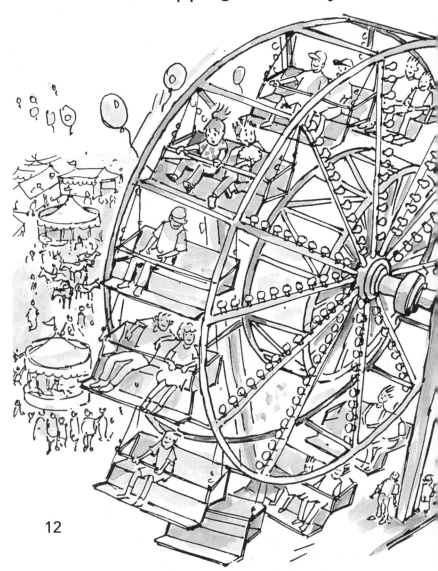

right up at the top. Matt calmly ate candy floss, but Gabby looked straight down and shuddered.

She looked quickly across the park to where the ponies were. From up in the sky they looked like fat little chairs.

"No pony rides yet," Matt said, even though Gabby hadn't said one word. "The haunted house comes next."

Chapter 4

There was a witch at the door of the haunted house, checking tickets. She had hair like grey cobwebs.

"I'd rather wait out here," Gabby said.

"You're coming with me," Matt said. "Mum said we had to stay together."

Gabby could hear spooky wails coming from inside. "There's a ghost in there!" she whispered.

"It's only someone's dad dressed up in a sheet. I'm not missing out on the haunted house just because you're so scared! Just follow me and you'll be OK."

Gabby knew the haunted house would be worse than the climbing wall and the ferris wheel!

She was right.

Chapter 5

Inside the haunted house it was as dark as midnight. Gabby had to feel her way along the walls. Cold winds blew around her feet.

The floor didn't stay still and doors weren't where she thought they'd be. Furry things tickled her neck.

"Keep moving," Matt said. "This is only the first room. If you just stand in the one spot, people can't get through."

There was a cupboard Gabby had to walk past. Only it wasn't a cupboard, it was a deep black hole in the wall …

"There are lots of kids behind us," Matt said. "They're all getting squashed because you're blocking the way."

There was something inside the
black hole ...

"Come *on*!" Matt hissed at Gabby over his shoulder. "Don't just stand there!"

A ghost floated out of the hole. It didn't look one bit like anyone's dad!

Gabby started screaming and couldn't stop.

Chapter 6

The ghost had to carry Gabby out the back door. Matt was hardly speaking to her now. He was too mad.

"You yelled so loudly even the poor ghost got a fright!" he said.

Gabby didn't know where to look. People seemed to be staring at her. She thought they must all know she'd made a big fuss inside the haunted house and had to be carried outside by the ghost.

"Matt, let's go and have a pony ride," she begged.

Chapter 7

But Matt kept finding other things to do instead. One of them was sticking his head through a hole and having wet sponges thrown at him.

Gabby, who didn't like getting water in her eyes, stayed out of the way. Matt went back for another turn.

Matt wasn't scared of *anything*, Gabby thought.

He even let a magician chop off his head!

"Don't do it!" Gabby whispered, but Matt was already jumping up on the stage.

Gabby kept her eyes shut until he came back down again in one piece.

Chapter 8

"We've just about run out of money now," Matt said. "But there's enough left for a ride on …"

"The ponies!" Gabby said happily.

"... the flying fox," Matt said. "I saved the best for last."

Gabby looked up the hill at the flying fox. It was even scarier than the one at last year's fair. The kids having turns on it were screaming much louder than she had screamed inside the haunted house. Just watching it made her feel dizzy.

She reached out and grabbed.

"Give that back!" Matt yelled. "Mum said *I'm* in charge of the money."

"She didn't say you're the boss of what we spend it on!" Gabby said.

"Come on, Gabby, you don't want a boring old pony ride."

"Yes, I do! And Mum said we had to stay together, so you'll just have to come with me."

Chapter 9

"No one's getting me up on a pony!" Matt said suddenly, in a voice that didn't sound much like his own. "I might fall off!"

"You wouldn't fall very far," Gabby said, staring at him in surprise.

"Ponies bite at one end and kick at the other!"

"Not the ones they bring to fairs."

"They shoot up in the air and buck people off!"

"Those ones wouldn't," Gabby said. "They're just like fat little chairs."

"I'll *hate* it!" Matt whispered, standing very still. His feet felt like two melted icy-poles, and he couldn't move.

Gabby reached out and took him by the arm.

"You'll love it," she said. "I'll go first. All you have to do is follow me."

Robin Klein

I wrote this story after going through a haunted house at a big school fair. The child I was with wasn't very keen to go in with me!

It was spooky inside! We lost each other in the dark, so I kept grabbing hands and saying, "Don't worry, I'll get us out of this!" (The hands all belonged to other children, who were very surprised!) Then, because I was holding everyone else up, a ghost came along and led me outside by *my* hand.

It was such fun that I think I'll go through that haunted house again next year!

Mike Johnson

Fairgrounds are fun, with lots of people and rides, but they can be a bit scary when you are small. The story of Gabby and Matt reminds me of something that happened to me when I was little. I loved horses, and I was always asking my mum and dad to let me have a pony ride.

One day, when I was riding at the beach, the saddle came loose and slipped around the pony's tummy. I slid around too, until I was nearly riding upside down! I was very scared!

I soon got over it, and I still love horses. (I like to draw them, too.)

More Solos!

Dog Star
Janeen Brian and Ann James

The Best Pet
Penny Matthews and Beth Norling

Fuzz the Famous Fly
Emily Rodda and Tom Jellett

Cat Chocolate
Kate Darling and Mitch Vane

Green Fingers
Emily Rodda and Craig Smith

Gabby's Fair
Robin Klein and Michael Johnson

Watch Out William
Nette Hilton and Beth Norling

The Great Jimbo James
Phil Cummings and David Cox